Heroes and Villains

Something Called A Sampo

by Geraldine McCaughrean 3

Illustrated by Heli Hieta

Robin and Marion

by Michaela Morgan 23

Illustrated by Michael Spoor

Mondamin

by Jan Mark 43

Illustrated by Graham Paslow

Rigby, Halley Court, Jordan Hill, Oxford, OX2 8EJ
a division of Reed Educational and Professional Publishing Ltd
www.rigbyed.co.uk

Rigby is a registered trademark of Reed Educational and Professional
Publishing Ltd

Heroes and Villains first published 2002

'Something Called A Sampo' © Geraldine McCaughrean 2002
'Robin and Marion' © Reed Educational and Professional Publishing Ltd 2002
'Mondamin' © Jan Mark 2002

Series editor: Wendy Wren

06 05 04
10 9 8 7 6 5 4

| *Heroes and Villains* | ISBN 0433 07802 2 |
| Group Reading Pack with Teaching Notes | ISBN 0433 07808 1 |

Illustrated by Heli Hieta, Michael Spoor, Graham Paslow
Cover illustration © Belicta Castelbarco 2002
Repro by Digital Imaging, Glasgow
Printed in Great Britain by Ashford Colour Press, Gosport, Hants.

SOMETHING CALLED A SAMPO

A story from the Kalevala
by Geraldine McCaughrean

CHAPTER 1
VAINA GOES WOOING

If you want to marry the most beautiful wife in the world, you must offer something special in exchange. Vaina racked his brains to think what that might be.

"Love! Offer her love!" said his brother Lemmin, clutching his heart.

"That will suit her," said his other brother Ilmarinen, "but her mother will want more."

So Vaina set off to woo the bride of his choice. Though he had never met her, his heart was set on the Maid of Pohjola, Princess of the BackCountry, far to the north, where everlasting winter gripped the land in claws of ice. Vaina was no longer young. In fact, he had been alive for almost as long as the world itself. But he could still sail and swim and sing and fight, and he was ready to do anything to win the Maid of Pohjola.

Steering towards the
colours that hung like streamers of
magic in the northern sky, Vaina was still
thinking about a suitable wedding present
when a frost giant, lying in ambush, leaped
out from behind a mountain. Whirling its
white body around Vaina, it whisked him off
his feet and flung him eight days out to sea.

Day and night Vaina swam, swallowing salt
water and spitting out fish, until at last,
gibbering with cold, he sighted land. Huge
copper rollers, built for the launching of
longships, edged the sea. His efforts to
clamber ashore set the rollers spinning, and a
dozen times he was dumped back into the
freezing sea. When he finally pulled himself
to his feet, his clothes tinkled round him, each
drip and trickle frozen into an icicle. He made
a strange sight, slinking and chinking his way
to the castle of Queen Louhi.

Vaina took heart as he looked around, for what girl would choose to stay in this dreary backwater of the world if she got the chance to leave it? The castle was gloomily dark, lit only by the flicker of blubber-oil lamps. Draughts chewed like rats at his ankles. The food on the table was whale and eel, eel and whale, whale and eel, and bear meat.

"Yes, I will give you my older daughter for a wife," said Queen Louhi, chafing her blue hands together, "if you can pay the price. Make me a sampo that will last from now until the last day of Forever."

Vaina accepted at once. Lesser men might have stopped to ask, "What IS a sampo?" Not Vaina. After all, his own brother was the best blacksmith in the world. There was nothing Ilmarinen could not make at his magic forge.

As he left the palace, drizzle was falling over the drab copper hills. For a moment, a watery sun broke through. Vaina looked up and saw a sight that made his old heart rattle around his chest. There sat the Maid of Pohjola on the slope of a rainbow, weaving cloth-of-gold out of sunlit rain.

"My, you're a bonny sight!" exclaimed Vaina. "Let's you and I get wed, lass! Then we can get out of this horrible hell-hole!"

The Maid looked at him, as pale and delicate as frost on a blade of grass. "Peel me a stone, and I *may* marry you."

Now it so happened that Vaina had brought with him for the journey a pocketful of cherries. He took one out now and split its ruby red skin, peeling the cherry stone. "No sooner said than done!"

"Chop me that woodpile without making one splinter, and I *may* marry you," said the Maid in a sleepy, sing-song sigh. The pile she pointed to was not of logs at all, but brittle, breakable ice.

Vaina crammed the ice inside his vest, and when it melted, he wrung the water out, letting it refreeze in little lumps which he tossed into the girl's lap. "I see you're keen, lass, or you'd set me a really difficult task!"

"Build me a ship out of this loom of mine, and I *may* marry you," was all the Maid said in her lilting Lappish language.

So Vaina began to sing. He had been singing since the dawn of the world, and his songs could make trees dance, rivers run uphill, and the copper mountains toss their heads. Piece by piece he transformed the loom into keel and hull, mast and tiller. The sails were cloth-of-gold.

"Now sail home, old man," said the Maid of Pohjola coldly, "and do as my mother asked ... or do you have too little magic down there at home in Kalevala to make a sampo?"

CHAPTER 2
THE BLACKSMITH STRIKES SPARKS

"Magic is not the problem," explained Ilmarinen. "You tell me what to make and I'll make it, before you can say 'fifty-five fresh fish'. But what IS a sampo?"

Lemmin shrugged. Vaina shook his head.

So Ilmarinen threw fuel into his furnace and heated it hotter than hot. Then he took lambswool, barley, milk and swan feathers – and fused them in the fire. Out of the furnace came a golden bowl, perfect and shining, but Ilmarinen did not want a bowl. So he smashed it and threw the pieces back into the furnace. After a time he opened the door and there lay a red copper ship, but Ilmarinen did not want a ship, and he broke it and threw the pieces back into the fire. The third time, he found a cow with golden horns, the fourth time a plough, but he threw them back into the furnace, heating it white-hot.

This time, out came a sampo.
A what?

A sampo. It is as good a
name as any for something that
never existed before and can never be made
again. It had three sides, one lid, and a little
handle, which turned without winding.

Armed with this marvellous, magical
wedding present, Vaina made the long
journey north to the BackCountry of Ice and
Dark to claim the Maid of Pohjola. Ilmarinen
the Blacksmith went too.

Queen Louhi took one look at the sampo
down the length of her icy blue nose, and
gave her blessing. The Maid took one look at
Ilmarinen the Blacksmith, and he got hers. "I
want to marry the blacksmith," she said in a
lovelorn whisper. And what with the magic in
the northern sky and the magnetism under
the northern earth, Ilmarinen felt the same.

Vaina wondered, should he rage and stamp about? Should he sing magic songs? Should he sulk? Instead he said, "What good is an unhappy wife to me? Marry her, brother, then let's get out of here."

Queen Louhi gave her daughter a kiss like a wipe with a wet rag, then forgot all about her. She told her craftsman to build a stronghold for the sampo: a copper cabin, and inside it seven rooms, one within the other, each door fastened with seven padlocks. In the innermost room, two giant guard dogs prowled the magic darkness. As for the sampo, well its three sides gleamed and its lid chinked and its little handle spun round and round. The magic mill had begun to grind and, left alone, would do so until the last day of Forever.

CHAPTER 3
RETURN TO THE BACKCOUNTRY

"What brings you here again?" asked Queen Louhi loudly, over the noise of birdsong. One year had passed.

The three heroes gaped about them. The castle hall was sunny and warm. Vases of flowers stood where, one year before, courtiers had shivered in sealskin cloaks and hats. Beyond the blowy curtains, a bright sun shone on fields plush with barley, on orchards ripe with fruit.

"I thought you said this place was black and cold," whispered Lemmin, who, this time, had travelled with his brothers.

"Before my sampo, it was," breathed Ilmarinen.

Even before reaching the BackCountry, they had seen signs of the sampo's magic. The fish in the seas around Pohjola had grown to an enormous size and their ship had collided with a giant pike: all scales and fins and teeth. Happily, the ship had sunk the pike and not the other way round.

Queen Louhi had to repeat herself. "What brings you here again? And where is my daughter?"

"There was an accident," said Ilmarinen. "Last month."

"Very sad," said Vaina.

"Very," said Lemmin, "except for the bears, I suppose."

Ilmarinen looked at the floor. The Evil Bears of Kullervo had eaten the Maid of Pohjola: a tragedy for her husband, and a shock for the bears, who found her as cold as a sliver of ice, as spiky as fishbones in their throats.

"She wasn't much more than a mouthful, either," Lemmin recalled, shaking his shaggy head.

Ilmarinen wiped his eyes with his beard. "That is why I've come back to ask for your other daughter."

"Huh!" laughed Queen Louhi. "I give you one girl and you feed her to the bears! What would you do with the other?" (She did not ask the Princess herself, who perched palely on the sunny window sill.) "Go home, men of Kalevala, before I give you my curse!"

If Ilmarinen could not have a bride, then he wanted his sampo back, but he knew that Louhi would never give it up. Its magic had transformed her dreary land into a paradise. He asked, instead, whether they could share the sampo.

Louhi wiped her sweaty armpits with her long hair. *"Can two puppies share one whine? You keep your luck; I'll keep mine."*

Vaina reached inside his coat and pulled out a ... something. After their ship's collision with the pike, Vaina had made its jawbone into a huge harp. Now he began to play.

Vaina had been making music since the dawn of the world, and his tunes could make porpoises somersault, birds fly upside down and the copper mountains lie down to sleep. Now it was the Queen who slept. Half risen from her chair, she slumped back, snoring like a walrus. Around her, every member of her court yawned and sank to the floor.

Ilmarinen caught the younger Princess as she fell, and slung her over his shoulder. On tiptoe, all three brothers ran to the copper cabin where the sampo was kept – seven rooms one within another and each one sealed with seven padlocks. Ilmarinen eased butter into the padlocks while Vaina went on crooning strange, wordless songs, plucking his strange, gaping harp. When the seventh door opened, they found the giant guard dogs draped over the sampo, asleep. The mill was still merrily grinding out wealth, plenty and happiness. In fact, the little room was so crammed with happiness that Lemmin burst out singing.

"Shshsh!" hissed the others. Lemmin's singing was not magical; it was not even tuneful but it was very, very loud. It boomed through the copper cabin and rang round the sleeping castle. Taking the sampo with them, the three heroes ran for the shore, shoved their ship across the copper rollers, and leaped to their oars. So hard did they pull that the keel leaped clear out of the water.

When the Princess awoke, she watched them sourly with small yellow eyes. She had no wish to leave a home knee-deep in wealth and happiness. As the ship reached deep water, she flapped her white, muscular arms, lifted her beaky nose, and rose into the air – a great white flapping gull. Ilmarinen watched her go.

"I'm sorry," said Vaina.

"A lucky escape, I think," said Ilmarinen. "Wives like that will eat every sardine in the house."

A noise like thunder told them that when they were in the castle, Lemmin's singing had indeed woken the sleepers. Even now, the Queen's ship was trundling over the copper rollers as large as a castle, a hundred men at the oars and a thousand standing.

CHAPTER 4
THE GREAT CHASE

The great ship was captained by the Queen herself, beating a drum and chanting curses, *"Come from the seabed, Fog and Mists! Wrap my enemy in your fists!"*

Instantly, Vaina's ship was shrouded in fog as thick as wool. They could not see their oars' ends, let alone the guiding stars overhead, or the reefs, whirlpools and icebergs in their path.

Vaina picked up the jawbone harp and played. Magically, the fog began to glow and trickle, to drip and drop into the ocean like honey trickling off a spoon. The air emptied of fog and the horizon reappeared, sharp as a wire. Even so, Louhi had made up ground. She beat on the ship's drum and chanted, *"Monstrous Kraken, rise and kill! Kraken rise and eat your fill!"*

Like a breaching whale,
a monstrous head rose from the sea in front
of Vaina's ship, jaws agape. Vaina rolled his
cloak into a ball and hurled it down the fish's
throat. Feeling a tickle on its tongue, the
Kraken snapped shut its jaws. Ilmarinen
snatched hold of its two frilled, fleshy ears,
hauling the brute up out of the sea, hanging it
from the mast by its nose. There it hung,
steaming in the sun, shedding a hail of scales.

The struggle, though, had cost precious minutes. Louhi was gaining fast. Now she summoned a magical storm. The sea rolled and writhed like a thousand krakens, and waves swamped the ship to its brim. Vaina could not catch his breath for long enough to sing, and when he took out the magic harp, it was dashed from his hands by a wave and plunged to the bottom of the sea!

Looking back, the heroes thought they saw a thundercloud. Looking back, they thought they saw an island. Looking back, they knew they were seeing a ship as large as any castle, one hundred men at its oars and one thousand standing. Suddenly, Louhi was upon them.

Vaina reached for his tinderbox. His wet fingers fumbled for a flint. As he flung the flint into the sea, he sang, *"Grow reef and crack their prow! Rise rocks and wreck them now!"*

The tiny flint grew to the size of a pebble, to the size of a stone. It multiplied a millionfold into a reef as high as the sky. Louhi's rowers dug in their oars and tried to slow, but the gigantic ship crashed headlong into the reef.

Clapping her arms over port side and starboard, the Queen called to her men to grab hold of her skirts. Then, like a bird built of timber and hemp and hair, she rose into the air – an eagle carrying a thousand men in her tail-feathers, a bird of prey swooping down on Vaina's floundering ship.

"It's mine and I shan't share it!" shrieked the witch-eagle, and, reaching iron talons into the ship, she snatched the sampo out of Ilmarinen's grasp.

Vaina was on his feet in a moment, lugging an oar from its rowlock, swinging and swiping. The oar's tip struck something, which spun away and dropped with a plop into the ocean.

"The sampo!" cried Ilmarinen.

"Ahhhhwwk!" shrieked Louhi. "I'll shoot down the sun for this! I'll burst the moon! I'll make you pay, you pirates of Kalevala!"

But then the winds beat her backwards, towards her own land, and the sea currents carried the heroes onwards towards theirs.

Only the polar star, rising that night, glinted on something bobbing among the waves: the lid of the sampo floating and drifting over the darkling sea. It washed up among the seaweed and shells of Kalevala's beaches, and from then on the harvest grew taller, the beasts fatter, the coffers fuller, the people happier than they had ever been before. Poets, above all, found the air swarming with words, and wrote the greatest verses in the history of Kalevala – songs of sampos, heroes and the sea.

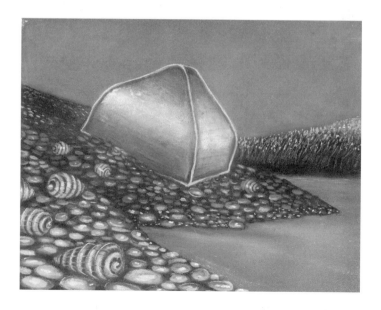

Robin and Marion

by Michaela Morgan

Chapter 1
~This Man Robin Hood~

A group of ragged townsfolk were gossiping in the market place of old Nottingham town.

"Well I say that so-called Robin Hood is nothing more than a common criminal," said one white-haired old man. "Laws are for keeping. He and his bunch of outlaw rogues have no respect for the laws of the land. A common criminal – that's all he is!"

"Rubbish!" said a bold woman. "The laws of this land are unfair. The Sheriff and his men are the rogues. They steal our money, they take our homes, they imprison us if we object. They can even kill us if they like! Where's the justice in laws like that?"

The crowd murmured their agreement and then a young girl piped up, "I don't think he's a criminal! And he's certainly not common. They say he's of noble birth."

"They say all sorts of things," said the old man, "but how much can we believe?"

"Well, I know one thing," one boy muttered. "He saved my father from the Sheriff. He's a hero!"

"Yes!" said his friend. "Every day there are new stories of his bravery. I heard that he—"

The old man interrupted, "Tall tales! Only fit for gullible peasants and children. Fairy stories!"

"Who would like to hear one of those tales?" asked a minstrel, seizing his opportunity. "Gather round and listen and I'll sing you the latest ballad of Robin Hood and his Merry Men."

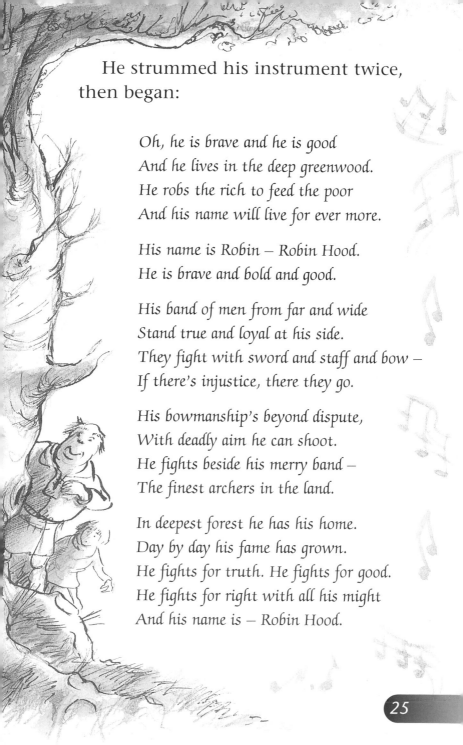

He strummed his instrument twice,
then began:

Oh, he is brave and he is good
And he lives in the deep greenwood.
He robs the rich to feed the poor
And his name will live for ever more.

His name is Robin – Robin Hood.
He is brave and bold and good.

His band of men from far and wide
Stand true and loyal at his side.
They fight with sword and staff and bow –
If there's injustice, there they go.

His bowmanship's beyond dispute,
With deadly aim he can shoot.
He fights beside his merry band –
The finest archers in the land.

In deepest forest he has his home.
Day by day his fame has grown.
He fights for truth. He fights for good.
He fights for right with all his might
And his name is – Robin Hood.

High above the minstrel, a man lurked in the branches of a tall oak tree. Dressed in green, with a hood covering his head, he was nearly invisible. He almost seemed to be part of the tree. His face was half in shadow. Then a sudden sunbeam, a small flash of light, illuminated him. If you were quick, if you were very quick, you could have caught a glimpse of the man they called Robin Hood.

Much later, when the minstrel had finished his song and the small crowd had dispersed, Robin Hood swung down from his tree-top perch. After his years living in the forest, he was at home among the branches. He could leap from bough to bough, as agile as a squirrel. Smoothly, he slid to the ground and disappeared back into the green darkness of the forest.

Chapter 2
~Under the Greenwood Tree~

That evening, Robin Hood and his band of outlaws were eating a hearty meal.

"I'm worried," said Robin.

"Why worry?" asked Little John. Little John was an oak tree of a man, strong, sturdy and enormous. Like the rest of the band, he was dressed from head to toe in green. Like the rest of them, he could blend into the forest in a trice.

He bit into a hunk of venison and beamed. "We have everything we need here – food, the shelter of the trees and good company. What is there to worry about?"

Robin shook his head sadly. "I was in town today. I heard how they are talking of us. They talk of little else. They even have ballads about us! They think I can solve all their problems, fight all their fights. They say I'm a hero but I know I'm just an ordinary man. I fear I will let them down."

"Never!" said Little John. "And you *are* a hero!"

"I am an ordinary man who has been forced into this wild way of life – an ordinary man in extraordinary times. That's what I am. If good King Richard had not gone away and left our country in the hands of his cruel brother King John, and rogues like the Sheriff of Nottingham, I could be living a happy, normal life – maybe with the Lady Marion." Robin Hood sighed deeply.

"Well, *now* I understand!" cried Little John. "You're lovelorn, that's what you are. It's time we paid a visit to the lovely Lady Marion!"

So it was decided.

Early next morning, when the dew was still on the grass, Robin and his band set off. The air was fresh and the sun sparkled on the leaves.

"Bless the Lord for another perfect day!" sighed Friar Tuck.

"Amen to that!" Little John agreed, and so did the rest of the band – Will Scarlet, Much the Miller's son, Allan A'dale … and Robin Hood himself.

All day the men tramped through the woods, heading for Gamley Hall, the fine home of Squire Gamley.

The Squire and his son, Will, had been lifelong friends to Robin. He had passed many a happy childhood day playing with Will, and with Marion, who had come to live at Gamley Hall. Marion's own family and home had been destroyed by cruel King John but the kindly Gamleys had given her a home and loved her with all their hearts.

Indeed, everyone loved her for her beauty, kindness and courage. Oh, it had been a sad time for her! She had seen her family and her beloved home taken away, but she had turned her sadness into strength. She had learned everything she could to make herself wiser and more powerful. She had even learned to shoot a bow and arrow. She was as good an archer as any of Robin's men.

Robin's sorrow lifted with every step that took him towards the Hall. But when he finally gazed down at his beloved Gamley Hall, his heart sank. Squire Gamley's flag had gone, and in its place the Sheriff's flag fluttered from the tower. The Sheriff had taken Gamley Hall for himself, bending the law to satisfy his greed. There were soldiers all around, but the Squire, Will and Marion were nowhere to be seen.

"What are we going to do?" It was Will Scarlet who spoke and it was Robin who answered.

"We wait till nightfall. Then we attack!"

Chapter 3
~The Uninvited Guest~

ittle by little the darkness fell and, blanket-soft, settled all around Robin and his men. The band stayed in the trees, camouflaged in green, cloaked in darkness. Then softly, at Robin's whispered signal, his men slipped out of the shelter of the leaves and one by one slid into the cool, murky waters of the moat. Silently, silently they swam across to the Hall and hid themselves all around it.

At the same time, Robin strode out of the forest. Making no attempt to hide himself, he marched briskly across to the main entrance of the Hall. Soldiers observed him and shouted to each other. Robin did not flinch. He marched up to the heavy oak door and rapped on it imperiously. "Ho!" he called. "Let me in. It is I! Robin Hood!"

Soldiers scattered and ran to inform their master of the uninvited guest at the door. The Sheriff was not in residence. He had given the Hall as a reward to one of his henchmen, Sir Guy of Gisborne.

Sir Guy was enjoying settling into his new home. He had all the servants running around him. They offered him rich food and fine wine – all stolen from Squire Gamley.

One of Sir Guy's men ran in and, bowing quickly, stammered, "There is a stranger at the gate, my lord. We think it is Robin Hood!"

"Ha! Come looking for his friends, has he?" sneered Sir Guy. "Well, he won't find them here!"

He thought for a moment. "Is the outlaw alone?" he asked.

"Yes, sire, he is," his servant answered.

A brilliant plan occurred to Sir Guy. What if he invited Robin Hood in to 'discuss' the taking of Gamley Hall? What if he then captured Robin and presented him to the Sheriff of Nottingham? Sir Guy knew that the Sheriff was desperate to catch Robin Hood and now here the outlaw was, within his grasp! The Sheriff would have a splendid reward for the friend who gave him such a prize!

"Open the gates!" Sir Guy commanded.

"Is that wise, my lord?" the servant asked.

"DO AS I SAY!" roared Sir Guy. "Check that the rogue is alone, first, of course. If he is, let him in. When he's safely inside, arrest him and bring him to me!"

The soldiers on the wall above the gate peered into the gloom. "He is alone," they confirmed to the men below. *CRRREEEAAK* ... one bolt was unfastened. *CRRREEEAAK* ... a second bolt was dragged back. The door swung wide and there stood Robin Hood, proud and alone.

But not for long! Soon leaves were thrown aside, shadows grew legs, whole bushes ran raging at Sir Guy's men. The soldiers tried to heave the heavy door closed, but too late. Robin Hood and his band were in! A bitter fight broke out as the soldiers tried to hold them back. Sword clashed against sword, staff against skull. Daggers flashed and arrows flew. Robin and his men fought their way to the great banqueting hall, where Sir Guy had been feasting.

Sir Guy and his men were fine swordsmen and the fight was evenly matched until Sir Guy lifted his sword high and hacked down one of the fiery torches that lit the hall. His men quickly followed his lead. Candles, torches, lamps all fell to their swords. Soon the hall was plunged into darkness.

Now all was confusion. Shadow fought against shadow, sword clashed against sword, but in disorder. Neither side could tell who was who. In the darkness, Sir Guy slipped away to safety.

Suddenly, there was a glow from the floor. Straw had caught fire and speedily, speedily it spread. Soon the roof timbers were rivers of roaring flame. Unable to see and hardly able to breathe, Robin's men retreated but Robin battled on. *Marion must be here somewhere …* he was thinking, but his thoughts went no further. CRACK! A burning beam snapped. CRASH! It fell from the ceiling. A glancing blow floored Robin. He lay unconscious as a wall of flame roared towards him.

Through the smoke, Little John saw what had happened. With one bound, he was back. He heaved the beam aside, lifted Robin, and carried him out into the cool night air and safety.

Chapter 4
~Homeless Again~

obin sat with his head in his hands. Below him lay the charred ruins of Gamley Hall. Around him his band shuffled in uneasy silence.

"Marion?" whispered Little John.

"Not a sign," sighed Friar Tuck. "She must have been imprisoned with Will. They would have had no chance of escape."

In the far distance, horses could be heard approaching.

"We have to go," Little John insisted gently. "That may be more of the Sheriff's men."

"Let them come," sighed Robin. "Leave me here. Save yourselves. Without Marion, I care not if I live or die."

The sound of horses was growing louder.

"Robin!" cried Much the Miller's son, who was standing guard.

"Robin!"

The outlaws ran off to investigate, but Robin sat on, despairing. Imagine how he felt when a hand touched his shoulder and a laughing voice said, "So here you are! We have looked everywhere for you!"

It was Will Gamley and Marion. Behind them, Robin's band were beaming huge, sunny smiles at each other.

The pair told their story. The soldiers had arrived to take the Hall. The Squire had refused to hand it over without a fight, and had been killed. Here, Will paused and Marion laid a comforting hand on his arm. In the confusion, Marion and Will had taken their chance and fled to look for Robin. Robin, meanwhile, had been trudging to Gamley Hall looking for them!

Friar Tuck blessed Marion and Will, Robin hugged them, and Little John picked them both up and swung them round in the air.

"So you see," gasped Marion, "I am alive and well, but" – she gazed down at the smoking ruins of Gamley Hall – "now I am homeless again."

"Me too," said Will Gamley, "but I know what I want to do. I want to join you, Robin, and live the life of a free man in the greenwood. I will be one of your Merry Men," he announced, "if you'll have me!"

"With pleasure, Will!" said Robin, and he clapped his good friend on the back.

"And I ... " said Marion, " ... I will join you too!"

The band gasped.

"No!" said Will Gamley. "No lady joins the outlaws!"

"It would be too hard a life for you," said Robin, kindly. "We have no soft beds or fine furniture in the forest."

"Do you see any soft beds and fine furniture in Gamley Hall?" snorted Marion, indicating the still-smoking ruins of her home.

"But it isn't a safe life for you, my child," said Friar Tuck.

"Was I safe in Gamley Hall?" asked Marion. "Was I safe in my own home? I was not! I would feel safer by far with you. I need no luxury other than fine friends and freedom and ... " she added with a fierce look, " ... I can shoot an arrow as well as any one of you!"

"But ... " said Robin, "there are no other ladies in the forest."

"Then I shall be the first!" Marion declared.

The band smiled but Friar Tuck shook his head. "No, my lady, as your spiritual advisor, I cannot allow it. It would not be fit for a lady to live alone and unmarried with a gang of outlaws. It cannot be allowed."

Robin cleared his throat. "Marion would not be alone with us," he said. "And as for unmarried ... " He dropped to his knee. "If you will have me, my lady, I would gladly marry you. Will you marry me?"

Marion smiled. "I will!" she said.

And she said it again a week later when the wedding ceremony took place.

"Will you take this man to be your lawfully wedded husband?" asked the Friar.

"I will," Marion said.

True, it was not an elaborate ceremony. There was no magnificent cathedral – just the boughs of the trees, that arched over the couple and looked as fine as any church roof.

There was no choir but the birds sang sweetly throughout.

The wedding guests were few, but all of the couple's closest friends were there, clad in Lincoln green, with their hearts full of gladness to see Robin and Marion joined in matrimony.

Little John had a smile that outshone the sun and he couldn't help saying to one and all, "I know they will live happily ever after. I *know* it. Fairy stories! Sometimes they *can* be true!"

MONDAMIN

An adaptation of Hiawatha by Jan Mark

On the shores of a lake so vast it seemed as
wide as the sea, lived Hiawatha, the Chief of
his tribe.

His father was the West Wind, his
grandmother Nokomis was the daughter of
the Moon, but he was a man, and lived as a
man among his people.

He never knew his mother, who died when
he was born. His father, the West Wind, did
not know his son. Hiawatha grew up with
Nokomis, his grandmother, who sang him
songs when he was a baby and told him
stories when he was old enough to talk.

"Look in the sky," Nokomis said. "What do you see?"

"I see lights," Hiawatha said.

"Those are the stars," Nokomis told him, "and see that biggest star of all? That is the comet Ishkoodah, racing through the night with his hair on fire."

Hiawatha gazed at the comet.

"Look at the lake. What do you see?" Nokomis asked.

"I see a big, round light coming up out of the water," Hiawatha said. "Is it the sun, swimming at night?"

"That is the moon's reflection," Nokomis said.

"What are those shapes on it?"

"Oh, what a story," Nokomis said. "Once there was a warrior who grew so angry with his grandmother that he threw her right up into the sky. There she is still, the old woman in the moon."

"I wouldn't do that to you," said Hiawatha.

"I know, I know," his grandmother said.

"What are those lights that dance in the winter, over the lake, to the north?" asked Hiawatha.

"Those are the spirits in their death dance, mighty warriors who died in battle."

"And that great white track overhead, what is that?"

"Oh, that is the path where the ghosts pass over," said Nokomis. "We must all walk that path some day."

When he grew too old for stories, Nokomis walked in the woods with her grandson, talking by day and whispering by night.

"What do you hear?" Nokomis said.

"I hear voices. Who is talking?"

"Those are the owls."

"What is that beast with the funny flat tail and the teeth?"

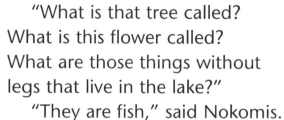

Nokomis told him, "That is the beaver."

"What is that tree called? What is this flower called? What are those things without legs that live in the lake?"

"They are fish," said Nokomis.

"Grandmother, who made all these things?"

"Gitche Manitou made the sun and the moon, the rain and the snow. He made the whole world and everything in it."

"Why did he make it?"

"He made it for us."

By the time Hiawatha became the Chief of his tribe he knew the name of every living thing. Nokomis had taught him all she knew, and Hiawatha had learned the most important thing of all. He had learned to ask questions.

Gitche Manitou, the Master of Life, had given the people all that he thought they would need to live on. The lake and the streams that fed it were swarming with fish; through the woods roamed deer; in the trees were pigeons and squirrels; overhead flew flocks of wild geese. Wild rice grew by the lakeside, grape vines and berry bushes stood thick with fruit. The people needed nothing more.

So they were hunters and gatherers, and most of the time they had more food than they could eat. But after dry summers the nuts were shrivelled, and the berries small and dry, and the birds and squirrels took them long before the people could. In hard winters the hunters went out for deer, but after days they came home with no more than a pigeon or a rabbit. When the great lake froze, a fisherman might sit all day by a hole in the ice, and catch nothing.

The tribe went hungry, and wondered if the Manitou had forgotten them.

Hiawatha heard what they said.

"No," he told them, "the Manitou does not forget us, but why should he remember us? He has given us everything."

As he said it, Hiawatha began to ask himself, *Is it true? Must we live like this?* But if things could be changed, he did not know how to change them.

It was the custom of the young men of the tribe to go alone into the forest and build a lodge of poles and birch bark. There they would fast for seven days and seven nights, waiting for dreams and visions to guide them through their lives. They would learn strength and wisdom from the spirits, drinking little, eating nothing, praying to become skilful hunters, cunning fishermen, courageous warriors, famous among the tribe.

That spring, Hiawatha went to the woods and built his lodge by the lake. He was a young man with his life before him, but he was not looking for skills and fame for himself. He was the leader of his people. Whatever he asked, he asked on their behalf.

On the first day of his fast he walked in the forest, away from the tracks and into the thickets. He trod so lightly that no creature fled from him when he came near it, so he saw the rabbit sitting at the mouth of its burrow, the squirrel on the branch, the roosting pigeons. He heard the cries of the wild geese overhead, and the pheasants in the undergrowth.

Everywhere he went he saw the beasts that his people hunted for food. At first he thought, *We have so much!* And then he thought, *But everything we have, we have been given*; and as he walked back to his lodge at nightfall he cried to the Manitou, "Master of

Life, is there nothing you have not given us?"

When he woke next morning, he left the lodge and wandered through the meadows beside the river. The grape vines grew over the trees, the wild rice was sprouting at the water's edge. With every step he took, he saw the new spring leaves, the buds that would be flowers in summer and berries in autumn. With every step he took, he saw the food that his people would gather through the coming year and he thought, *We have so much!* And then he thought, *These things grow by themselves, we did not put them here.* As he walked back to his lodge, he called to the Manitou, "Master of Life, can we do nothing for ourselves?"

He was young and strong and healthy, but at dawn the next day, when he woke, he had not eaten for two days and nights. He did not walk that morning, but sat by the lake as great as the sea, and watched the fish leaping in the sunlight, slipping like shadows beneath the surface, while the crawfish scuttled on their claws in the shallows.

He thought, *We have only to walk into the water and our food is all around us.* Then he thought, *How can we say this food is ours when all we have to do is reach out and take it?* And he cried to the Manitou, "Master of Life, must we depend on you for everything?"

On the fourth day he was too weak to step outside the lodge. As the sun rose, he lay on his bed of leaves and gazed out at the shining lake where the light slid and slithered on the ripples. And while the sun swung overhead, the shadows crawled across the floor like serpents. The rustling leaves sang in his head, and the lake's horizon rose and fell like a tide.

When the sun rolled into the lake, he did not know whether he woke or slept, where was up and where was down. His eyes were full of burning sky.

Then the shimmering dazzle died away, and out of the sunset someone came walking. Hiawatha raised his head and saw a slender young man dressed in green and yellow, with nodding green plumes of feathers in his hair. As the man stood in the doorway of the lodge, Hiawatha saw the strangest thing of all.

Hiawatha's hair was black like the hair of all his people. But this man's hair was long and silky, and in the last of the light Hiawatha saw that it was golden yellow.

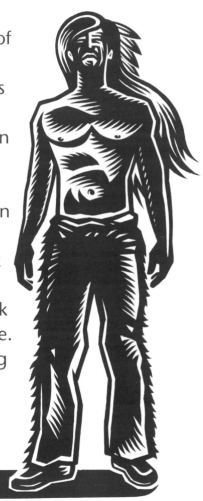

The golden-haired young man looked down at the black-haired young man who lay on his bed of leaves and said, "Hiawatha, the Manitou has heard you and listened. You did not ask to be a great hunter, or a clever fisherman, or a mighty warrior. You did not ask to be famous so that your name would be remembered until the world ends. You thought only of your people, so the Manitou has sent me to you.

"I am not a gift. I am your friend and my name is Mondamin. I have come to tell you how you shall have what you asked for, and how you must earn it. Stand and wrestle with me."

Hiawatha had not thought that he could even sit up, but he found the strength to stand, and stepped out into the fading sunset to wrestle with the stranger, Mondamin. No sooner had he laid hands on Mondamin's shoulders than he felt his strength return, as if his heart were pumping bright new blood around his body, and as the red and yellow blanket of the sky grew dark, the two men wrestled, but neither could throw the other down.

Then Mondamin spoke in the darkness. "That is enough for now. Sleep tonight and rest tomorrow, and when sunset comes, I will be here again."

On the fifth day of his fast, Hiawatha lay and waited for night to fall. Had he dreamed about Mondamin? Had he dreamed about the wrestling? How could he have wrestled with anyone – he could scarcely raise his head.

But as the sun went down, Mondamin stood again in the doorway of the lodge and said, "Here I am, Hiawatha. Stand up and wrestle with me."

Against the sunset sky the two young men, the dark-haired and the golden-haired, fought to gain the victory. But each was as strong as the other, and neither could win. As darkness fell, Mondamin vanished, and all that night and all next day Hiawatha lay in his lodge as the moon and the stars and the sun spun round him and he wondered, *Did I dream it?*

On the sixth evening, Mondamin came again and for the third time they wrestled: struggling, stamping, sweating, until the sunset had passed. Then Mondamin stood shining in the last of the light and said, "You have fought me three times and you have proved that you deserve to win. Tomorrow is the seventh and last day of your fast.

Tomorrow, we shall wrestle together for the last time. Tomorrow, you will win and I shall die.

"This is why I came to you, and I am ready for death. Now I shall tell you what you must do. When I am dead, dig a grave for me where the rain will fall and the sun will shine. Take off my clothes and my green feathers and lay me naked in my bed. Cover me with earth and let it lie lightly on me.

"Through spring and summer, watch by my grave. Drive away the birds and pull up the weeds. Do this alone, Hiawatha. Do not forget me, and soon, I will wake and live again."

Hiawatha slept that night, and in the morning of the seventh day his grandmother Nokomis came with food. "Eat," she begged him. "You have fasted too long. Have I brought you up only to see you die before I do, before you have a wife and children?"

Hiawatha smiled and said, "No. No, I must not eat, and no, I shall not die. Go home and wait for the end of this seventh day. And take away the food." Hiawatha was afraid he would be tempted to eat, for he was now so weak and exhausted that he wondered if Nokomis might be right, and he would die before the day ended.

That evening, there stood Mondamin, golden in the sunset, and Hiawatha dragged himself upright and staggered from the lodge to meet him, for the last time.

For the last time they faced each other; for the last time they wrestled, and as the setting sun turned the forest to fire and the lake to flame, Hiawatha stood alone and Mondamin lay dead at his feet.

Hiawatha wanted only to sleep, but he remembered his promise to Mondamin, and remembered that the Manitou had sent him. With a hoe made of shell he scraped out a grave. With weary hands and aching shoulders, he stripped off the green and yellow clothes, and the plumy feathers, and laid Mondamin in his resting place. He heaped the earth over him and let it lie lightly upon him.

Then Hiawatha left his lodge, and, through the dark woods, beneath the stars, he went home to Nokomis.

His fast was over, he had called to the Manitou, he had seen his visions, and he did not forget Mondamin. Every day, while the sun shone or the rain fell, Hiawatha went back to the grave and watched beside it. The green and yellow garments and the nodding plumes were fading like withered leaves. He tended the soil and pulled out the weeds. He drove away the birds and he waited to see Mondamin live again.

One day, he saw that a pale green feather was growing out of the grave. Then there was another, a third, a fourth. Soon, Mondamin's plumes of feathers stood where the golden-haired young man lay buried.

As summer drew on, tall stalks grew out of the grave, bearing leaves as green as the clothes Mondamin wore, and in autumn came great golden seeds. From each cob of seeds hung a tassel of silky yellow hair, and Hiawatha cried, "Mondamin! Mondamin lives again!"

Then he gathered the people of the tribe together and took them to the grave to tell them how, in a vision, he had wrestled with Mondamin.

"And here he is," Hiawatha said. "Mondamin stands where I buried him. He is maize, he is sweet-corn, and the Manitou sent him to us."

Someone said, "The Manitou sends us everything. What is so special about this maize, Mondamin?"

Hiawatha said, "You know and I know that our food is all around us. Often, there is plenty but sometimes there is nothing, and when there is nothing, what can we do about it? We go without. We starve. We die. But we can do something about the maize. This will be our food if we work to grow it, and what we do not eat we must save, for Mondamin does not live forever.

"Each year, as summer ends, Mondamin will die. When spring comes, we must take the golden seeds and bury them as I buried Mondamin. We must lay the earth lightly over them, pull up the weeds all summer long, and drive away the thieving birds.

"If we do this faithfully, then every year, for ever more, Mondamin will live again."